BERTIE

Based on *The Railway Series* by the Rev. W. Awdry

Illustrations by
Robin Davies

EGMONT

EGMONT

We bring stories to life

First published in Great Britain in 2005
by Egmont UK Limited
239 Kensington High Street, London W8 6SA
This edition published in 2008
All Rights Reserved

HiT entertainment

ISBN 978 1 4052 3474 0
1 3 5 7 9 10 8 6 4 2
Printed in Italy

The Forest Stewardship Council (FSC) is an international, non-governmental organisation
dedicated to promoting responsible management of the world's forests. FSC operates a
system of forest certification and product labelling that allows consumers to identify
wood and wood-based products from well managed forests.

For more information about Egmont's paper buying policy please visit www.egmont.co.uk/ethicalpublishing

For more information about the FSC please visit their website at www.fsc.uk.org

*T*his is a story about Bertie the Bus. Bertie and Thomas both think they can go fastest. They just can't agree, so they decide to have a race to settle the argument once and for all …

One day, Thomas was waiting at the junction when a bus came into the yard.

"Hello," said Thomas. "Who are you?"

"I'm Bertie. Who are you?"

"I'm Thomas. I run this branch line."

"Ah – I remember now," said Bertie. "You were stuck in the snow. I took your passengers, and Terence the Tractor pulled you out. I've come to help you with your passengers today."

"Help me?" said Thomas crossly. "I don't need any help. Anyway, I can go faster than you."

"You can't," said Bertie.

"I can," huffed Thomas.

"I'll race you," said Bertie.

Their drivers agreed to the race.

"Are you ready?" said the Stationmaster. "Go!"

And they were off ...

Thomas always had to start off slowly, and Bertie was soon ahead of him. But Thomas didn't hurry.

"Why don't you go fast? Why don't you go fast?" called Annie and Clarabel anxiously.

"Wait and see! Wait and see!" hissed Thomas.

"He's a long way ahead, a long way ahead," they wailed.

But Thomas didn't mind. He remembered the level crossing.

Bertie was there, waiting impatiently at the gates while Thomas and his carriages went sailing through.

"Goodbye, Bertie," called Thomas.

After that, the road left the railway, so Thomas, Annie and Clarabel couldn't see Bertie. Then they had to stop at a station to let some passengers off.

"Peep, pip, peep! Quickly, please!" called Thomas.

Everybody got out quickly, the Guard blew his whistle and off they went again.

"Come along. Come along," sang Thomas.

"We're coming along. We're coming along!" sang Annie and Clarabel.

"Hurry! Hurry! Hurry!" panted Thomas.

Then he looked ahead and saw Bertie crossing the bridge over the railway, tooting triumphantly on his horn!

"Oh, deary me! Oh, deary me!" groaned Thomas.

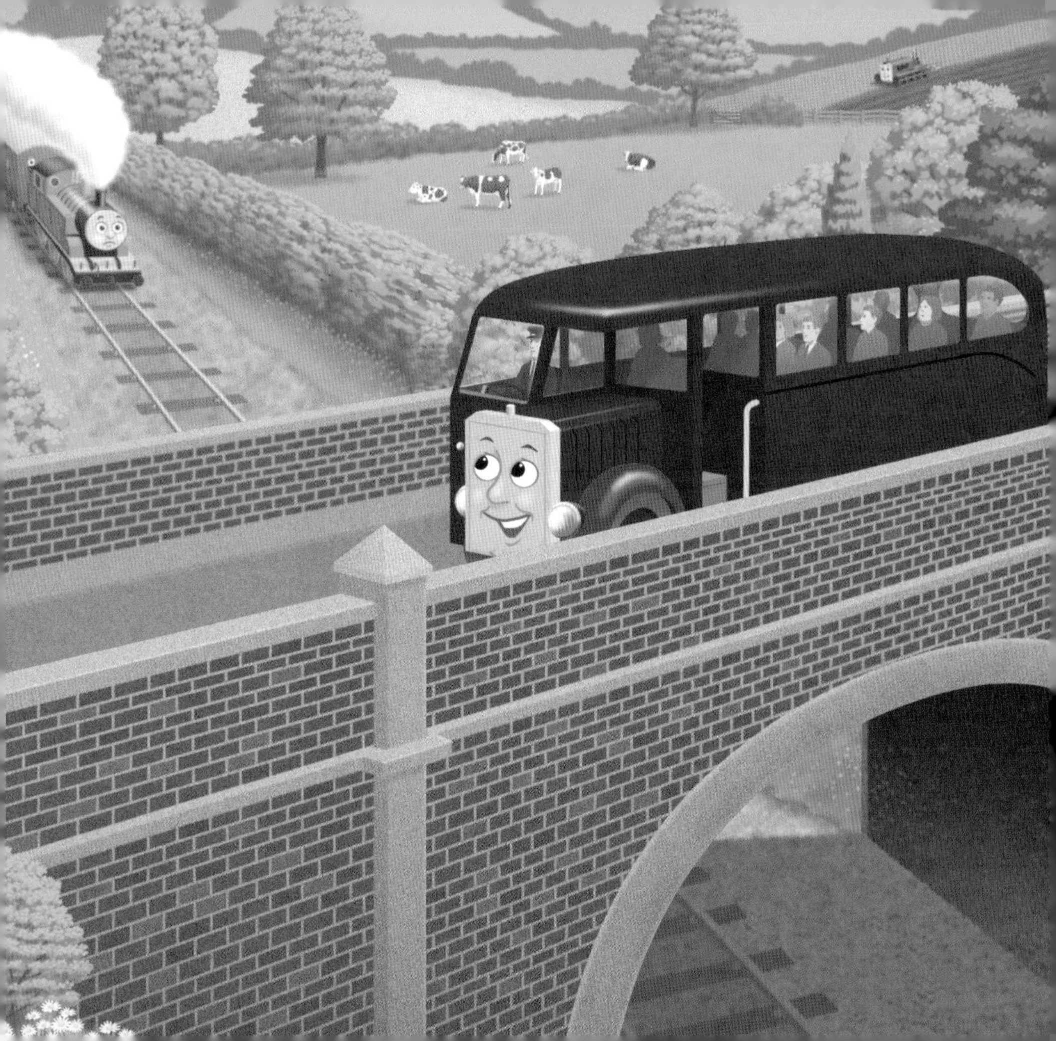

"Steady, Thomas," said his Driver. "We'll beat Bertie yet."

"We'll beat Bertie yet. We'll beat Bertie yet," echoed Annie and Clarabel.

"We'll do it. We'll do it," panted Thomas. "Oh, bother, there's a station."

As Thomas stopped, he heard a toot.

"Goodbye, Thomas," called Bertie. "You must be tired. Sorry I can't stop – we buses have to work, you know. Goodbye!"

The next station was by the river. They got there quickly, but the signal was up.

"Oh, dear," thought Thomas. "We've lost!"

But at the station he had a drink of water and felt much better.

Then the signal dropped.

"Hurrah, we're off! Hurrah, we're off!" puffed Thomas happily.

As Thomas crossed the bridge, he heard an impatient "Toot! Toot!"

There was Bertie, waiting at the traffic lights.

But as soon as the lights changed, Bertie started with a roar, and chased after Thomas.

Now Thomas reached his full speed. Bertie tried hard, but Thomas was too fast.

Whistling joyfully, he plunged into the tunnel, leaving Bertie far behind.

"I've done it. I've done it," panted Thomas.

"We've done it, hooray! We've done it, hooray!" chanted Annie and Clarabel, as they whooshed into the last station.

The passengers all cheered loudly. When Bertie came in, they also gave him a big welcome.

"Well done, Thomas," said Bertie. "That was fun, but I would have to grow wings like an aeroplane to beat you over that hill!"

Thomas and Bertie now keep each other busy. Bertie finds people who want to travel by train and takes them to Thomas, while Thomas brings people to the station for Bertie to take home.

They often talk about their race. But Bertie's passengers don't like being bounced around like peas in a pan, and The Fat Controller has told Thomas not to race at dangerous speeds.

So although (between you and me) they would like to have another race, I don't think they ever will. Do you?

The Thomas Story Library is THE definitive collection of stories about Thomas and ALL his friends.

5 more Thomas Story Library titles will be chuffing into your local bookshop in August 2008!

Jeremy
Hector
BoCo
Billy
Whiff

And there are even more Thomas Story Library books to follow later

So go on, start your Thomas Story Library NOW!

A Fantastic Offer for Thomas the Tank Engine Fans!

Cut along the dotted line

In every Thomas Story Library book like this one, you will find a special token. Collect 6 Thomas tokens and we will send you a brilliant Thomas poster, and a double-sided bedroom door hanger! Simply tape a £1 coin in the space above, and fill out the form overleaf.

TO BE COMPLETED BY AN ADULT

To apply for this great offer, ask an adult to complete the coupon below and send it with a pound coin and 6 tokens, to:
THOMAS OFFERS, PO BOX 715, HORSHAM RH12 5WG

☐ Please send a Thomas poster and door hanger. I enclose 6 tokens plus a £1 coin. (Price includes P&P)

Fan's name..

Address..

....Postcode...............................

Date of birth..

Name of parent/guardian...

Signature of parent/guardian..

Please allow 28 days for delivery. Offer is only available while stocks last. We reserve the right to change the terms of this offer at any time and we offer a 14 day money back guarantee. This does not affect your statutory rights.

☐ Data Protection Act: If you do not wish to receive other similar offers from us or companies we recommend, please tick this box. Offers apply to UK only.

Cut along the dotted line